# Haunted hoax or real-live ghost?

"What are you doing?" Jason asked, watching her write.

"She's getting ready to solve the mystery," George answered for Nancy. "Just wait— Nancy will figure out what's happening in the woods if anyone can!"

"Cool!" Jason grinned. "Hey Nancy, if you catch a real ghost, maybe we'll all be on TV."

Nancy looked up at him. "I won't be catching any ghosts," she said. "There's no such thing. But if something is going on to make people think the woods are haunted, I want to find out what it really is."

## The Nancy Drew Notebooks

Available from Simon & Schuster

# THE
# NANCY DREW
# NOTEBOOKS®

#62

*The Secret in the Spooky Woods*

## CAROLYN KEENE
ILLUSTRATED BY JAN NAIMO JONES

Aladdin Paperbacks
New York   London   Toronto   Sydney

First Aladdin Paperbacks edition October 2004
Copyright © 2004 by Simon & Schuster, Inc

ALADDIN PAPERBACKS
An imprint of Simon & Schuster
Children's Publishing Division
1230 Avenue of the Americas
New York, NY 10020

The text of this book was set in Excelsior.

Printed in the United States of America.
10 9 8 7 6 5 4 3 2 1

NANCY DREW, THE NANCY DREW NOTEBOOKS, and colophon
are registered trademarks of Simon & Schuster, Inc.

Library of Congress Control Number 2004102673

ISBN 0-689-87413-8

# 1

# Some Spooky News

"I wish, wish, wish I could go see *Spook Story* this weekend," George Fayne moaned.

Nancy Drew smiled at her best friend. "I know," she said as she gathered up her books and jacket from the classroom closet. It was the end of the day on Friday, and everyone was getting ready to go home. "Too bad our parents said we're not allowed."

Nancy's other best friend, Bess Marvin, shivered. "There's no way I'd ever see a movie like that no matter what my parents said," Bess declared. "It sounds way too scary!"

Nancy, Bess, and George were all eight years old and in Mrs. Reynolds's third-grade class. In lots of other ways, though, they were all very different from one another. For one thing, they looked different. Nancy had reddish-blond hair, while Bess's hair was blond, and George's was dark brown. They also had very different opinions about scary movies. George loved them. Bess hated them. Nancy just thought they were silly.

The girls' classmate Jason Hutchings heard what Bess said. "What's the matter, Bess?" he teased. "Are you a 'fraidy cat?"

His friends David Burger and Mike Minelli started chanting, "'Fraidy cat, 'fraidy cat!" over and over again.

Bess's cheeks turned pink. "Quit it!" she cried. "I'm not a 'fraidy cat. I just don't like ghost movies!"

Mike grinned. "If you don't like ghosts, you'd better stay away from the park," he told Bess.

"What do you mean?" Nancy asked curiously.

Jason shrugged. "Everyone knows the park is haunted."

The boys rushed away before Nancy could ask any more questions. Nancy, Bess, and George walked toward the door more slowly. They stepped into the hall.

"I wonder why he said that," Nancy said. "I've never heard about the park being haunted."

"I have!" Lindsay Mitchell spoke up. She was right behind them with her friend, Jennifer Young.

George wrinkled her nose at Lindsay. "Were you listening to our conversation?" she asked. Lindsay was famous around school for being a gossip. She liked to know what was going on at all times, and she liked to tell people about whatever she found out.

"It's okay, George," Nancy said. She wanted to know what Lindsay had heard. Nancy didn't believe in ghosts, but she thought it was strange that people were saying the park was haunted. Nancy loved to solve mysteries. Her father, Carson Drew, said she was a natural detective.

Lindsay tossed her long hair over one shoulder. "Everyone's talking about it," she declared. Her voice got low and spooky. "They say there are strange noises and creepy lights in the woods behind the playground."

"That's right," Jennifer added. "I heard that even the police are afraid to go in the woods now! Like Lindsay said, everyone is talking about it."

George frowned. "*Everyone* isn't talking about it," she said. "Nancy and Bess and I didn't know anything about it until now."

"That's probably because we haven't been to the park for a few days," Bess pointed out. She wrapped her arms around herself, looking nervous. "And if there are ghosts there, it's a good thing!"

"There's no such thing as ghosts," Nancy assured her friend.

Lindsay shrugged. "It sure looked like ghosts to me," she said. "I saw some weird blue lights flashing in the woods yesterday."

"Really?" Nancy said thoughtfully. "I'm sure there must be some normal explanation. All someone has to do is figure it out."

George grinned. "Uh oh," she joked. "It

sounds like Nancy is getting ready to solve another mystery!"

"You'd better not try," Jennifer warned with a shudder. "It's too dangerous!"

"She's right, Nancy," Bess whispered, sounding scared. "Ghosts are nothing to mess around with!"

"Hey, Jennifer!" a voice called.

Nancy turned around and saw Brenda Carlton hurrying toward them. Brenda was in their class too. She had red hair and a bossy personality. Her father ran the local newspaper, and Brenda had started a school newspaper of her own called the *Carlton News*. She wrote all the stories herself and printed it on her computer.

Jennifer looked over at Brenda. "What?" she asked, not sounding very friendly.

"I heard you just got a new puppy," Brenda said eagerly. "Can I interview you so I can write an article about it for my newspaper?"

"You're going to write a whole article about someone's dog?" George asked.

Brenda frowned. "I have to," she mumbled. "I don't have enough stories for the next

edition. Nothing ever happens around this boring town!" She stared at Jennifer. "So what's your puppy's name?"

"Princess," Jennifer replied. "She's a toy poodle."

Brenda started scribbling notes on the pad she was holding. "Does she bark a lot?" she asked.

Lindsay giggled. "Princess barks all the time," she said. "At least, she barked the whole time I was at Jennifer's house last Saturday. She's really cute, though!"

"My dog, Chip, used to bark a lot when she was smaller," Nancy said. "But we taught her not to."

Just then Alison Wegman came rushing up to the group. "Hey," she said. "Why are you guys talking to *her*?" She pointed at Brenda.

"Do you mind? I'm trying to interview Jennifer for the *Carlton News*," Brenda whined. She suddenly looked very upset.

"Well, mind your own business from now on!" Alison said nastily. "Come on, you guys."

She grabbed Jennifer and Lindsay by

their arms and dragged them off down the hall. Brenda watched them go, still looking upset. Then she stomped off in the opposite direction without a word to Nancy or the others.

"That's weird," Nancy said. "I thought Alison and Brenda were best friends."

George shrugged. "I heard they had another fight."

"Oh," Nancy said. There was no mystery about that. Alison and Brenda were always fighting and making up. "Well, that's one mystery solved. But that leaves another one—those so-called ghosts at the park."

"Don't remind me!" Bess wailed. "Just thinking about it is going to give me nightmares."

George looked grumpy. "Thinking about ghosts just reminds me I'm not allowed to see that movie," she said. "So what are we going to do today instead?"

Nancy grinned. "I have a great idea," she said. "Let's go to the park!"

# 2

# At the Park

I can't believe we're at the park!" Bess moaned, sounding scared. "I can't believe you guys talked me into it!"

"Oh, be quiet, Bess," George said. "Does this place look scary to you?"

Nancy, Bess, and George were walking into the park. Their parents had all given them permission to go there as long as they were home before dinnertime. It was a nice day, and there were lots of people out enjoying themselves, including plenty of kids from school. Nancy was holding Chip's leash. Chocolate Chip was Nancy's Lab puppy, and she loved going for walks in the park.

Nancy looked around carefully. A bunch of middle-school kids were sitting under the big maple tree. On the playground, a few kids from Nancy's elementary school were playing on the swings and the monkey bars. Nearby, Brenda Carlton was getting a drink from the water fountain. Jason Hutchings and five or six other boys were playing soccer on the big, grassy field between the playground and the woods.

Everything looked perfectly normal. But Nancy knew that didn't always mean everything *was* normal.

She patted her jacket pocket, checking to make sure her special blue notebook was there. Her father had given it to her. Whenever she was working on a mystery, Nancy liked to write down all her clues inside it. She still wasn't sure if the ghost stories were a real mystery, but she wanted to be prepared—just in case.

"Come on," she said. "Let's go over and check out the woods."

Bess shuddered. "No way!" she cried. "I'm

not going into those woods. Not when there may be ghosts in there!"

Nancy could tell her friend was really scared. "All right," she said. "How about if we go talk to Jason and the other boys? Maybe they saw something mysterious."

Chip barked loudly. She was staring at the soccer ball the boys were kicking around.

George giggled. "Chip says yes," she said. "Come on, let's go!"

The three girls and the dog ran toward the soccer game. The closer they got, the harder Chip pulled on her leash. Her tongue flopped out of her mouth, and she barked loudly.

"Stop it, Chip," Nancy cried. "You can't run off."

The boys heard Chip's bark. Jason looked over as the girls reached the edge of the field.

"Hey, look," he called to the other boys. "Nancy brought a *real* dog."

Mike Minelli laughed. "Yeah," he said. "Not like that wimpy little dog Jennifer was walking earlier."

"You mean Jennifer Young?" Nancy said.

She had a good memory. She remembered what Jennifer had said earlier, even though she hadn't been paying that much attention. "I heard she got a poodle puppy."

"It looked more like a fluffy little mouse to me," Jason joked. He bent down and patted Chip. She licked his hand happily. "Your dog is cool, though. Can she play soccer?"

"Sure," Nancy said. "She loves it!"

"Cool!" Peter DeSands called. "Let her off the leash so she can play!"

Nancy hesitated. One of the park rules was that all dogs had to be under control. Because Chip was still a puppy, Nancy usually kept her on her leash.

"Well, okay," she said after a second. "I guess she won't run off if there's a soccer ball around."

She snapped off Chip's leash. The boys cheered. Jason kicked the ball, and Chip barked and raced after it.

"Look, she loves it!" George said.

Nancy smiled. "I know. But help me keep a close eye on her, okay? I don't want her to run off or anything."

Her friends nodded. Nancy watched Chip carefully for a minute or two. But then her eyes wandered toward the woods beyond the field. Even though it was a bright day, the woods looked dark and a little spooky. Could there really be ghosts in there?

Nancy shook her head. She didn't believe in ghosts.

"Hey." Jason Hutchings ran over to them, breathing hard. He flopped on the grass and looked back at the game. The other boys were still playing with Chip. "Your dog is awesome, Nancy."

Nancy smiled. "Thanks. I think so too."

Jason looked over at Bess. "You should be afraid of Chip, Bess," he said with a smirk.

"Why?" Bess looked confused.

"Everyone knows that dogs love to chase 'fraidy cats!" Jason burst out laughing at his own joke.

Bess frowned and stared at the ground. She looked upset. But she didn't say anything.

George rolled her eyes. "Grow up, Hutchings," she said.

Jason shrugged. "Whatever," he said. "I

just thought you girls might not like to sit so close to the woods." He pointed toward the trees. "That's where all the ghostly stuff happens, you know."

Nancy decided it was time to start solving this mystery. If she proved there were no ghosts, maybe the boys would stop teasing Bess.

The first thing she wanted to do was figure out exactly what was happening in the woods. "What did you see?" she asked Jason. "Why do you think the woods are haunted?"

"Well, I didn't see anything," Jason replied. "But Laura McCorry told me she was walking near the edge of the woods when she heard someone moaning. When she turned to look, all she saw was a shadowy figure floating up through the treetops."

Bess gasped. "Really?"

"Uh-huh." Jason nodded. "And Alison Wegman said she was walking down the main trail two days ago when she heard footsteps behind her." He lowered his voice. "But when she turned around, no one was there!"

Nancy pulled out a pencil and her note-book. She opened to a fresh page.

She wrote "The Secret in the Spooky Woods" at the top.

Below that, she wrote down what Jason had just said.

Clues:
   1. Shadowy moaning figure (Laura M.)
   2. Spooky footsteps (Alison W.)

"What are you doing?" Jason asked, watching her write.

"She's getting ready to solve the mystery," George answered for Nancy. "Just wait— Nancy will figure out what's happening in the woods if anyone can!"

"Cool!" Jason grinned. "Hey Nancy, if you catch a real ghost, maybe we'll all be on TV."

Nancy looked up at him. "I won't be catching any ghosts," she said. "There's no such thing. But if something is going on to make people think the woods are haunted, I want to find out what it really is."

"W-what else could it be?" Bess asked.

Nancy looked down at her notebook. Then she looked over at the woods.

"I don't know," she said. "That's what makes it a mystery. But I don't believe in ghosts."

George looked over Nancy's shoulder at her notes. "That stuff sounds pretty ghostly," she said uncertainly. "What else could it be?"

"Well, it could be someone trying to scare us by making up stories," Nancy said, looking over at Jason. She knew he liked to tease people.

"Hey, it's not me!" he protested. "Everything I said is true. I heard it all from Lindsay today."

"So that only leaves one possible answer." Bess wrapped her arms around herself and shuddered. "Real ghosts!"

Jason shrugged. "I think the 'fraidy cat is right," he said. "I bet those woods are the home of an ancient burial ground. Or maybe a crime site!" He grinned at Bess. "Hey, 'fraidy cat, why don't you go in there and find out?"

Bess frowned. Before she could answer,

there was a shout from the direction of the soccer game.

Nancy looked over and let out a gasp. "Chip, no!" she cried.

But her puppy didn't look back. Barking eagerly, Chip ran off the soccer field—and straight into the woods!

# 3

# Doggone Scary

**N**ancy shoved her notebook back in her pocket and ran after Chip. George and Bess followed. They were all calling the puppy's name. But Chip disappeared into the woods without slowing down.

"Oh, no!" Bess cried as she ran. "What if the ghosts called Nancy's dog toward them? They could have her already!"

"You're right!" George panted. "I saw that happen in a late-night movie on TV once. Only it was a bunch of chickens, not a Lab puppy."

All three girls skidded to a stop at the edge of the trees. Nancy was sure that ghosts had nothing to do with Chip running into the woods. But she was still worried.

"I don't know what would make her run off like that," Nancy said, peering into the dim woods. There was no sign of her puppy. "Soccer is practically her favorite thing. Even a rabbit or squirrel running by wouldn't distract her from that."

"S-s-so what are we going to do now?" Bess asked, sounding very nervous.

Nancy took a step into the woods on the main trail. "We've got to find her," she said. "Come on!"

George followed her right away, taking a few steps down the trail and calling Chip's name again. Bess was scared, but after a moment she agreed to come too.

"Good luck," Jason called from the field. The soccer game was already starting up again. "Say hi to the ghosts for me!"

"P-promise we're just going to find Chip, then come right out again," Bess said to Nancy in a quavering voice. "We're not going to hang around looking for clues or anything!"

"All I care about right now is finding my puppy," Nancy said, walking a little faster.

The wide trail was made of packed dirt and went winding between the tall trees. There were lots of roots sticking out everywhere, which meant the girls had to watch their step. They walked side by side, deeper and deeper into the woods.

"Do you see any pawprints?" George asked, looking down at the ground in front of them.

Nancy looked too. "I don't think we'll be able to see any," she said. "The ground is pretty hard and dry."

"Plus, if the ghosts are carrying Chip, she wouldn't leave any footprints," Bess said with a shiver.

George pointed ahead of them. "Hey, look at that," she said. "It's a fork in the trail. I don't remember that being there."

Nancy looked where her friend was pointing. She had walked down this trail about a month earlier on a nature hike with her dad. "You're right," she said. "It wasn't. I remember seeing it there, but that second trail was all overgrown. I remember

21

because Dad called it 'impassable,' and at first I thought he was saying 'impossible.'" She giggled. "Then he said it was both!"

"That's weird." Bess stared at the new trail. "I wonder if the ghosts cleared it?"

"Don't be silly," George told her cousin. "Ghosts don't use trails. They can just float through trees and stuff, remember?"

Nancy whistled loudly. "Chip!" she called. "Chip? Where are you?"

*Wrrruff!*

George gasped. "Did you hear that?"

"Uh-huh!" Nancy's heart jumped. She recognized that bark! "Chip!" she yelled again. "Hey, Chip!"

*Wrrruff! Wrrruff!*

*Yip!*

Nancy blinked. "Chip?" she called uncertainly. The first few barks had sounded normal. But why was the last one so high-pitched and weird?

"Was that her?" George asked in surprise.

Nancy shrugged. "Maybe," she said. "I hope she's not hurt or something."

"Maybe it wasn't her at all." Bess's eyes were wide and scared. "Maybe it was a ghost dog! That could be what lured her away—Chip loves other dogs, remember?"

"I think the barks are coming from that way." Nancy pointed down the newly cleared trail. "Come on, let's find her."

They ran down the trail. It had even more twists and turns than the main trail. Nancy called to Chip several more times, and each time the answering barks got louder. The small yips were still mixed in with normal barks.

"We're getting close," Nancy cried. "Hurry!"

A moment later they rounded another turn in the trail. There was a clearing just ahead. Chip was trotting across it, coming straight toward them!

"Chip!" Nancy raced forward and grabbed her puppy in a big hug. "Are you okay?"

Chip licked Nancy's face. Her tail wagged back and forth.

"She looks okay," George said. "Maybe she was just scared. That's probably why her barks sounded strange."

"Or maybe the ghost dog is here right now," Bess whispered, staring around the clearing. "It could be invisible!"

Nancy didn't believe in ghost dogs any more than she believed in any other kind of ghost. She was just happy that Chip was safe and sound.

She realized she had left the puppy's leash back on the soccer field. She grabbed Chip's collar.

"Come on," she said. "We'd better go back and—"

Before she could finish her sentence, laughter poured out of the woods nearby. It sounded muffled, but very loud. A second later a big, round rock rolled out of a clump of bushes and right across the clearing in front of the girls!

"It's the ghosts!" Bess shrieked. She turned and raced back down the trail at top speed.

George and Nancy followed her. "Bess, wait!" Nancy yelled, still holding onto Chip's collar as the dog ran beside her. Her heart was pounding. She might not believe in ghosts, but that laughter sounded pretty spooky. "Slow down!"

But Bess didn't slow down at all until she was out of the woods by the soccer field.

She was panting and trembling when Nancy and George caught up to her.

"D-d-d-did you s-s-see that?" Bess cried. "Did you h-h-hear that spooky laughter?"

"What happened?" Jason ran up to them, followed by the other boys. "Did you see any ghosts?"

Nancy was already looking for Chip's leash. She wanted to make sure her puppy didn't run off again before she did anything else.

"Hey!" a man's voice shouted loudly from somewhere nearby. "What are you kids doing? That dog needs to be on a leash!"

Nancy looked up and saw a tall, thin man hurrying toward them with an angry expression on his face. He stopped just a few yards from Nancy and Chip.

"You there," he said loudly, pointing at Nancy. "That mutt has to be on a leash at all times!"

"I'm sorry," Nancy said. She was surprised by how angry the man looked. She finally found Chip's leash and picked it up in her left hand. She was still holding the puppy's collar with her right hand. "I didn't

know that was a park rule. I'll remember from now on."

The man scowled at her. Chip barked at him and wagged her tail. Without a word, the man spun on his heel and stomped away into the woods.

"Wow," Bess said. "Who was that guy? He seemed really mad."

"That's Mr. Garrison," Mike Minelli spoke up. "He's the new park ranger. He just started working here last weekend."

Jason nodded. "Yeah," he said. "He hates kids. He's always yelling at us and trying to ruin our fun. He almost made Jennifer Young cry yesterday."

"Why would he get a job at the park if he hates kids?" George wondered.

"I don't know, but it's true." A fourth-grader named Greg Karoli stepped forward. "He lives two doors down from me. One time my sister and I were playing Frisbee with our next-door neighbor's dog in their backyard. We accidentally tossed the Frisbee too far and it went in Mr. Garrison's yard. He came out and said if we did it again, he was going to call the police!"

"Bummer," Nancy said. "The park should have someone nicer working for it."

She hoped the new park ranger wouldn't spoil all their fun. Maybe he would be more pleasant if they all followed the rules. She decided that from now on, she would always keep Chip on her leash at the park.

Just then Nancy remembered that she was still holding the leash in one hand and Chip's collar in the other. As the other kids kept talking about the new park ranger, she bent over to attach the leash to the collar.

As she did, she noticed that something was wrapped around Chip's collar. It looked like a folded piece of paper.

She pulled it loose and unfolded it. There were a few words written on it in spidery-looking handwriting. Nancy gasped when she read them.

"What is it?" George asked, hearing her.

Nancy held up the slip of paper. "There was a note on Chip's collar," she said. "It says, 'Stay out of the woods—or else!'"

# 4
# Mean Mr. Garrison

T hat proves it!" Bess cried. "It was the ghosts!"

Nancy had to admit that for a second, back in the woods, she had wondered if ghosts might be real after all. But now that the moment of fright was past, she was thinking more clearly. She was sure that someone—a person—was definitely behind all the "ghostly" behavior.

"Come on," she told her friends, tucking the note into her notebook to examine later. "It's getting late. We need to go home for dinner."

\* \* \* \*

A little later, Nancy was sitting at the dinner table in her house playing with the lima beans on her plate. Her father was sitting at the head of the table. Hannah Gruen was sitting across from Nancy. Hannah had been the Drews' housekeeper since Nancy was three years old.

Hannah and Nancy's dad were talking about a case at Mr. Drew's law office. Normally Nancy loved hearing about her father's work. But at the moment she wasn't listening. She was still thinking about the spooky encounter at the park.

"Are you okay, Pudding Pie?" Mr. Drew asked. Pudding Pie was his favorite nickname for Nancy.

"I'm okay," Nancy said. "I was just thinking about something that happened today."

"What's that, Nancy?" Hannah asked, helping herself to more potatoes.

"Bess and George and I were talking to some kids at school," Nancy explained. "They said the park was haunted."

"Haunted?" Mr. Drew raised one eyebrow in surprise. "Why do they think that?"

"Some kids say they saw weird lights or

heard noises and footsteps," Nancy said. "At first I thought they were just making up stories to scare Bess."

Mr. Drew chuckled. "Poor Bess," he said. "Did you tell her ghosts aren't real?"

"I tried," Nancy said. "But then when we went to the park after school, something happened. I think I have a real mystery to solve."

She went on to tell her father and Hannah everything. She tried not to leave anything out. Her father was always telling her to pay attention to details, and that's what she did when she was working on a case.

"Hmm," Mr. Drew said when she finished the story. "Very interesting, Nancy. It sounds like Bess really believes there are ghosts in the woods. Do you believe that's possible?"

Nancy thought for a second. A lot of strange things had happened—Chip running off, the spooky laughter, the mysterious rolling rock. In some ways, it really did make sense to think that ghosts were behind it all.

But finally she shook her head. "No. I don't believe in ghosts," she said. "I think it might be someone pretending to be a ghost."

Hannah smiled. "Smart girl," she commented, standing up to carry some empty dishes to the kitchen.

Mr. Drew looked pleased too. "Then all you have to do is figure out who's trying to scare people. Who do you think would do something like that?" Mr. Drew said.

"Well, it could be Jason and his friends from school," Nancy said, twirling her spoon between her fingers. "They like to play pranks on people, especially girls."

Hannah returned from the kitchen just in time to hear her. "That sounds like a good answer to me," she said, taking her seat at the table. "Those boys are full of mischief."

Nancy was thinking about the boys. "It was Jason who started talking about the ghosts at school," she remembered. "And he was at the park later. But how could he have made those spooky noises and written that note I found on Chip's collar? He was

33

playing soccer the whole time I was in the woods."

"Maybe it was one of his friends," Mr. Drew suggested.

Nancy shrugged. "Most of them were playing soccer too," she said. "Wait! Except for David Burger—I don't remember seeing him. Maybe he was hiding in the woods waiting for us."

"Sounds like a good theory to me," Hannah said.

Nancy stared at her almost-empty plate. She still wasn't sure what to think about her new mystery. Maybe the boys had done it. But if so, how had they gotten Chip to run into the woods? And how had they known that Nancy and her friends would come to the park that day at all?

"Well, whoever did it, they almost got me in big trouble," Nancy said. "There's a new park ranger, Mr. Garrison. He was really mad about Chip running around loose."

"Do you mean Hank Garrison?" Hannah smiled. "Oh yes, that's right—he told me he was starting his new job at the park."

"You know him?" Nancy asked in surprise.

Hannah nodded and took a sip of water. "He's in my garden club," she said. "He's a wonderful man—very kind and thoughtful, with a terrific sense of humor."

"Maybe we aren't thinking of the same person," Nancy said. She couldn't imagine such a grumpy man even smiling, let alone having a good sense of humor. "Do you know if he maybe doesn't like kids?"

Hannah seemed surprised at the question. "Hmm . . . I'm not sure," she said. "He and his wife don't have any of their own— just a few pet birds, I think. But I've never heard him say a bad word about kids. Why do you ask?"

Nancy shrugged. "He didn't seem very friendly today when we saw him, that's all," she murmured.

She thought back to the angry look on Mr. Garrison's face. It just didn't match what Hannah was saying at all.

*Weird,* Nancy thought. *Just like this whole case.*

* * * *

35

The next morning Nancy called Bess and George to see if they wanted to go to the park again. The girls agreed to go. It was Saturday, so they had all day to work on the mystery. This time she decided to leave Chip at home.

As they walked toward the park, Nancy told her friends about her dinner conversation with her father and Hannah. "Maybe the boys are doing it," she said. "I wrote their names down on my suspect list."

She stopped in the middle of the sidewalk and pulled out her notebook. She showed her friends the page where she'd written down her list of suspects. It read:

Suspect #1: Jason and his friends
(trying to scare girls)

"Is that the only suspect we have?" Bess asked, reading the short list. "I don't think it counts as a list if there's only one person on it."

"That was all I could come up with yesterday," Nancy said. "But I spent all last night thinking about the case, and I might have one more suspect to add."

She pulled a pen out of her pocket and wrote down another suspect:

Suspect #2: Brenda Carlton

"Brenda?" George said. "Why her?"

"I was trying to figure out who could have sneaked into the woods after us," Nancy explained. "I thought about everyone we saw when we got to the park. Then I tried to remember everyone we saw when we came out of the woods."

"I saw Brenda when we first got there," Bess said. "She was over at the water fountain."

Nancy nodded. "Right," she said. "But I don't remember seeing her later."

"Are you sure?" Bess asked. "Anyway, why would Brenda want to scare us?"

George gasped. "I know!" she cried. "The *Carlton News*. She was just saying how boring it is around here these days. Maybe she's trying to make people think the park is haunted so she can write about it!"

Nancy smiled. "That's exactly what I was thinking," she said. She added another note to her list so it read:

Suspect #2: Brenda Carlton (needs exciting story for *Carlton News*)

They started walking again and soon reached the park entrance. "Are we forgetting anybody?" Nancy asked as they walked through the gates. "Who else would want people to think the woods are haunted?"

Before her friends could answer, there was a shout. "Hey! You there!"

Nancy looked up and saw Mr. Garrison hurrying toward them. Once again, his face was angry.

"What's he so grumpy about this time?" George whispered.

Mr. Garrison didn't hear her. He stopped in front of them, his fists clenched at his sides. "I told you, no dogs off the leash!" he yelled. "Where is that mutt of yours? It better not be running around loose again!"

"Don't worry," Nancy said quickly. "I didn't bring Chip with me today. She's at home."

"Oh." Mr. Garrison scowled. "Good. I hope that means at least one of you kids understands that rules are there for a reason." He shook his head and muttered under his breath, "Course, my job would be a lot easier if I didn't have to deal with kids who don't understand that."

He turned and hurried off without waiting for an answer. Nancy, Bess, and George stared at each other in surprise.

"That was weird. Sounds like he really doesn't want kids in the park," Bess said.

Nancy nodded and pulled out her notebook. "You're right," she said. "And I think we just found ourselves another suspect!"

# 5

# Poodles and Clues

**A**s Nancy wrote Mr. Garrison's name on her suspect list, she heard Bess squeal with delight.

"Look!" Bess cried. "What an adorable puppy!"

Nancy looked where Bess was pointing. On a grassy spot near the old maple tree, Jennifer Young was sitting on the ground playing with a cute little poodle puppy.

"That must be the puppy she was talking about at school yesterday," George said.

They hurried over. "Hi, Jennifer," Nancy said. "Is that Princess?"

"Uh-huh." Jennifer grabbed the playful

puppy and held her up. "Isn't she cute?"

Nancy reached out carefully to pat Princess. The poodle puppy was much smaller than Chip had been when Nancy first got her. Princess's eyes looked like tiny, shiny black buttons. Her paws ended in tiny little claws. Her wriggling, moist nose was tiny. Even the sparkly pink barrette Jennifer had attached to the curly hair on top of Princess's head was tiny.

"She's so sweet!" Bess told Jennifer, tickling the poodle pup under her chin. "I love her."

"Thanks." Jennifer smiled. "So are you guys here to look for more ghosts? Jason told me one chased you out of the woods yesterday. That must have been so scary!"

Nancy frowned. "Jason said that?" she said. "Well, I still don't believe it was a ghost. I think it was a person."

"Really?" Jennifer said. "I don't know, it sure seems like ghosts to me." She glanced around the park, which was filled with people, including lots of kids. "But maybe you're right. Come to think of it, I saw Brenda Carlton hanging around the edge of

the woods a little while ago." She pointed to Brenda, who was sitting on a bench over near the playground.

"Brenda?" Nancy repeated. She traded a look with Bess and George. This sounded like a clue! "Tell me more."

Jennifer shrugged and scratched Princess under the chin. "I didn't see much. She was by herself, and kept stepping into the woods and then right back out again. Then that mean new park ranger came and chased her away."

"Interesting." Nancy pulled out her notebook and wrote down "Brenda hanging around near the woods by herself" on her clues list. "Sounds like we should look into this a little more."

"Are you sure, Nancy?" Bess said. She was staring toward the soccer field. Jason and his friends were there again, kicking a ball around and shouting happily. "I still think it's probably those boys."

"What boys?" Jennifer asked. She followed Bess's gaze. "You mean Jason and Mike and those guys?"

George nodded. "They're the first ones

who told us about the ghosts," she said. "We think they might be trying to scare people as a joke."

"That makes perfect sense! You're probably right." Jennifer shrugged and set Princess back down on the grass. "Mystery solved. The best thing to do is to ignore them—if you just act like you don't care anymore, they'll stop soon enough, right?"

"I guess," Nancy said. "*If* they're the ones doing it."

"Oh, I'm sure they are," Jennifer said. She kneeled down beside her puppy. "Hey, check this out—I'm trying to teach Princess some commands. She's a really fast learner. Yesterday she learned 'come' in less than an hour. I used my new dog whistle." She pointed to a silver whistle hanging on a string around her neck. "Today we're working on a different command. SIT, Princess! SIT!"

The tiny puppy jumped up and down and barked. Even her bark was tiny—it sounded like she was saying *Yip! Yip!* Then she rolled over on her back.

Bess giggled. "That's cute."

"When I started training Chip to sit, she did the same thing," Nancy told Jennifer. "It helps if you push on their back end a little bit when you say the command."

Just then there was the sound of loud giggling and talking from nearby. Nancy glanced over her shoulder and saw four girls from class walking into the park. Alison Wegman was in the lead, chattering with Lindsay Mitchell. Just behind them were Sarah Churnichan and Laura McCorry.

As the four of them stopped just inside the park entrance and looked around, Nancy saw quick movement out of the corner of her eye. Glancing toward the playground, she saw Brenda Carlton jump up from the bench where she was sitting. Brenda hurried straight toward the girls.

"Hey, guys!" she called loudly.

Alison stared right at her. Then she spun on her heel and started marching away. "Come on, girls," she called loudly. "I feel like singing, don't you?"

"Definitely!" Lindsay and Sarah chorused, while Laura nodded.

The four of them started singing. Nancy didn't recognize the song, but Brenda seemed to know it. Her face fell, and then she scowled.

"What are they singing?" Bess whispered curiously.

Nancy shook her head, trying to listen. She couldn't hear all the words very well—the other girls were too far away. "It sounds like 'long live the FFC' or something like that," she said.

"The FFC?" George repeated. "What's that?"

Jennifer scooped up her puppy and stood up. "Oh, don't pay any attention to them," she said, looking rather uncomfortable. "They're just kidding around. That song doesn't mean anything—no big deal."

She tucked Princess under her arm. Then she hurried off toward Alison and her friends. A moment later she was walking with the other girls, and the song had stopped.

Nancy looked at Brenda. She was still standing by herself near the entrance. She stared after Alison, Jennifer, and the others,

46

looking embarrassed and angry. As Nancy watched, Brenda spun on her heel and stomped off toward the playground.

"That was sort of strange," Nancy commented. "Looks like Brenda and Alison are still fighting."

"Probably." George shrugged, not sounding very interested.

"Nancy! Hey, Nancy Drew!"

Nancy looked up to see who was calling her name. She saw Jason Hutchings, Mike Minelli, and David Burger running toward her.

"Hi," she said as they skidded to a stop in front of her. "What's up?"

David flopped onto the grass, panting from the run. "We were hoping you would come to the park today," he said.

"Yeah," Mike added. "We have a clue for your mystery."

"You mean the ghost stuff?" Nancy said. "What is it?"

"We all got prank phone calls last night," Jason said. He pointed to himself and the other two boys. "A few of the other guys did too."

"What kind of prank phone calls?" George sounded suspicious.

Nancy didn't blame her. Jason and his friends were famous for making prank phone calls. They even made them on each other.

Still, she figured she should listen, just in case it really was a clue. "What do you mean?" she asked.

"The phone rang last night right after dinner." Jason lowered his voice. "When I picked it up, all I heard was this loud, ghostly howl."

"A howl?" Bess leaned forward, her eyes as wide as saucers.

Jason nodded. "But that's not all," he went on. "I said, 'Who is this?' and that's when someone—or some*thing*—spoke back." He took a deep breath. "A spooky voice moaned, 'Beware of the haunted woods!'"

# 6

# Back to the Woods

**N**ancy wasn't sure whether to believe the boys' story or not. "You all got the same phone call?" she asked.

"Uh-huh," Jason said, and the other boys nodded.

Nancy looked at her friends. George shrugged. Bess just looked scared.

"You'd better write this down, Nancy," Bess said. "It's a clue!"

Nancy opened her notebook. Then she looked at the boys again. Were they teasing her? She still couldn't tell. But she decided to write down their story—just in case.

She added the spooky phone calls to her

clues list. "Are you sure you're not making this up?" she asked the boys.

"No way!" Jason said.

Mike nodded. "You can ask my brother Carl if you want," he said, pointing to a teenage boy getting a drink at the water fountain nearby. "He was sitting right next to me when I got my call."

Mike's older brother, Carl, heard his name and wandered over. Carl was seventeen years old and in high school.

"Hey, squirt," Carl said to Mike. "Did you call me?"

Nancy smiled at the older boy. "Hi, Carl," she said. "Mike was just telling us about the prank phone call."

"Oh, yeah!" Carl nodded. "That howling noise was freaky—and loud. It sounded like a ghost or something."

"Did you hear what the caller said after the howls?" Nancy asked.

Carl nodded again. "It said to beware of the haunted woods," he said. He laughed. "Poor Mike was so scared he dropped the phone and ran out of the room."

Mike looked embarrassed. "Be quiet, Carl,"

he mumbled as his friends started laughing.

"Anyway, it sounded pretty scary," Carl said. "But it was probably just one of these goofballs." He pointed to Jason and David.

"Thanks," Nancy said. She glanced at her friends. "Come on, you guys, let's go sit on the swings."

Carl wandered back toward his high school friends, while Jason and David kept teasing Mike about being scared. Nancy, Bess, and George left them behind and went over to the swingset on the playground. There were three empty swings side-by-side, and the girls sat down in them.

"Do you think those boys were telling the truth?" George asked, scuffing her feet in the dirt beneath her swing.

Nancy shrugged. "I don't know," she said. "I didn't at first. But why would Carl lie about it? If he said Mike got a spooky phone call, it's probably true. But that doesn't mean it was a ghost calling."

"It doesn't mean it wasn't," Bess argued. "I still think the woods could really be haunted."

"Maybe," George said. "Or maybe it is the

boys, and they're trying to scare each other now with those silly calls."

"Maybe," Nancy agreed. "But I'm not so sure anymore that the boys are the best suspects. They all looked pretty scared when they were telling us about the phone calls."

"Then who do you think is doing everything?" Bess asked.

Nancy was still holding her notebook. She let her swing rock back and forth as she looked down at the page.

"I'm not sure," she said. "We have a lot of clues, but I still can't figure out the answer."

She read over her whole page of notes again.

The Secret in the Spooky Woods
Clues:
1. Shadowy moaning figure (Laura M.)
2. Spooky footsteps (Alison W.)
3. Chip runs away from soccer game into woods
4. Spooky laugh and rolling rock in woods

5. Note on Chip's collar: STAY OUT
   OF THE WOODS—OR ELSE!
6. Brenda hanging around near woods
   by herself
7. Spooky phone calls (Jason, Mike,
   David, other boys)

Suspects:
Suspect #1: Jason and his friends
   (trying to scare girls)
Suspect #2: Brenda Carlton (needs
   exciting story for *Carlton News*)
Suspect #3: Mr. Garrison (maybe
   doesn't like kids in the park)

George leaned toward Nancy on her
swing and read over Nancy's shoulder. She
pointed to Brenda's name.

"Maybe it is Brenda," George suggested.
"She's always causing trouble. And she's
been acting kind of different lately."

"That's true," Nancy said. "We already
know she needs an exciting story for her
newspaper. Besides that, she seems like
she's really mad at Alison Wegman right
now."

George's brown eyes widened. "That's right!" she said. "Maybe she's trying to scare Alison."

Nancy read over the list again. "We should also pay attention to Mr. Garrison," she said. "Jennifer said he chased Brenda away from the woods this morning, remember?"

"Yeah," George said. "And it seems like he wants to stir up trouble for all the kids in the park. Maybe he wants to scare us away completely so we won't bother him."

Nancy nodded thoughtfully. She still remembered what Hannah had said about the new park ranger. But she also remembered the angry look on his face the two times he'd talked to Nancy and her friends.

"He's a good suspect," Nancy said. "He's always at the park, and it would be easy for him to do most of the scary stuff people are talking about. Easier than for most kids, anyway."

Bess tossed her hair back and pumped her swing a little, swooshing back and forth. "I still think you two are forgetting some very important suspects," she said.

"Real ghosts! All the stuff that's happening would be easiest of all for them!"

Nancy sighed. "All right," she said. "I guess I should write down all the possibilities."

She added another entry to the suspect list:

Suspect #4: Real ghosts

"I still don't believe in ghosts, though," she told Bess. "Besides, why would a ghost use the phone?"

Bess shrugged. "Why not?"

Nancy sighed. No matter how much they talked about it, she couldn't settle on one suspect. She decided it was time to start snooping around for real.

"Come on," she said, standing up. "Let's go investigate."

Bess looked nervous. "What do you mean?"

"We need some more clues," Nancy said. "We've got to go back into the woods."

She tucked her notebook into one of her pockets. Then she reached into her other one and pulled out a flashlight.

"See?" she said with a grin. "I'm prepared

this time. Even though the sun's still out, the woods get pretty dark."

Over Bess's protests, Nancy led her friends toward the woods. They entered on the same main trail.

"Hey! Where are you going?" Jason called to them from the soccer field.

"Are you ghost hunting?" David added. "Whoooooo!"

The girls ignored them. They continued on into the woods.

"What are we looking for?" George asked.

Nancy shrugged. "Anything suspicious," she said. "I want to go back to that clearing where we found Chip yesterday."

Bess gasped. "You mean where we heard the ghosts?" she squeaked, sounding scared.

Nancy nodded firmly. "That's the best place to look for clues."

They hurried down the trail until they reached the clearing. Bess hung back at the edge, staring around fearfully. Nancy snapped her flashlight on and starting searching the edges.

"Do you remember which way that rock rolled from?" she asked George.

George pointed. "I think it was over there."

The two of them hurried toward the spot. Nancy shined her flashlight on the ground. There was a stream nearby, and the ground was a little muddy in the whole area.

"D-do you see anything?" Bess called. She walked carefully toward them, still keeping a careful lookout for ghosts.

Suddenly she let out a yell of surprise. When Nancy looked over her shoulder, she saw that Bess was staring at the ground nearby.

"What is it?" Nancy asked.

Bess pointed. "Footprints!" she cried.

# 7

# Sneaky Sneakers

Nancy and George raced over to join Bess. "Where?" Nancy cried.

Bess pointed again. This time Nancy saw the footprints. There were two of them, right in the middle of a muddy spot. She aimed her flashlight at them for a better look.

"Sneaker prints," George declared, leaning closer. "Small ones—kid-size."

Nancy sighed. "That doesn't narrow things down much," she pointed out. "Most kids wear sneakers to the park."

"True," George said. "But it means Mr. Garrison didn't do it."

"You're right," Nancy agreed. "Unless he was chasing whatever kid left these prints. Didn't Alison Wegman say she heard someone behind her in the woods the other day?"

"I guess." George shrugged.

Nancy leaned closer, still looking at the prints. "Hey," she said suddenly. "Check it out. These prints are from two different brands of sneakers!"

She pointed. The print on the left had straight treads. The one on the right was decorated with swoops and swirls.

"That's weird." George leaned closer too. "It looks like they were left by someone wearing mismatched sneakers."

"Maybe we should go back out to the park and find out who has sneakers like that," Bess suggested. She still sounded nervous.

Nancy smiled at her. "Don't worry, Bess," she said. "I think these footprints probably mean there are no real ghosts around here."

"Right," George agreed. "I've never heard of a ghost wearing sneakers. Especially mismatched ones."

Bess giggled. "You're probably right," she

said. "Still, these woods are awfully spooky. Anyway, all we have to do is find someone wearing mismatched sneakers, and the mystery will be solved. Right?"

"Maybe," Nancy murmured. She was staring into the woods beyond the clearing. Were there more clues waiting in there? She had a feeling they might be getting close to the truth. "Let's just look around here a little more, okay?" she said to her friends.

They finished investigating the clearing, but they didn't find any more clues there. Next they followed the trail out of the far side of the clearing. Nancy kept her flashlight on and shined it on the ground as she walked.

"How come you are using the flashlight, Nancy?" George asked her. "There's plenty of light on this part of the trail." She gestured upward. Sunlight was filtering through the treetops, making it easy to see where they were going.

Nancy moved her flashlight beam back and forth on the ground. "The ground is pretty dry here," she said. "I thought the flashlight might make it easier to spot more footprints in the dirt."

"Oh," George said. "I guess that makes sense."

As they walked around a bend in the trail, the moving flashlight beam sparkled off of something at the edge of the trail just ahead—but it definitely wasn't a footprint.

"What was that?" Bess asked, blinking. "It looked like something shiny."

Nancy moved the beam until she saw the small flash again. She leaned over and picked up the shiny object. "It's a barrette," she said, holding it up for her friends to see.

"Is it a clue?" Bess asked.

"Maybe," Nancy said. "The 'ghost' could have dropped it."

"That would mean the ghost is a girl," George pointed out. "Like Brenda!"

Nancy shook her head. "I don't think so," she said. "She's got long, thick hair, remember? This barrette is way too small for hair like hers."

"Hmm," Bess said, thinking. "I guess that

means the 'ghost' has thin hair, right? I wonder who it could be?"

Nancy tucked the barrette carefully in her pocket. "I don't know," she said as they walked on. "Maybe there's another suspect we haven't thought of yet."

"It could be older girls," George suggested. "Someone we don't know, even. Or—"

Suddenly a loud, ghostly scream ripped through the woods. All three girls jumped, startled.

"Wh-what was that?" Bess gasped.

"LEAVE THESE WOODS AT ONCE," an unearthly voice howled, seeming to come from all around them, "OR THE GHOST OF THE PARK WILL GET YOU!"

# 8

# Ghosts Busted!

**B**ess screamed again and again as the ghostly words echoed around them. Then there was another loud howl.

Her heart pounding, Nancy stared at George. George looked very pale. Nancy still didn't believe in ghosts—but she was a little scared.

The echoes of the last howl faded away. Just then Nancy heard something else.

"What was that?" she asked.

Bess grabbed her by the sleeve. "Come on," she wailed. "We've got to get out of here before it's too late!"

Nancy shook her arm free. "No, wait," she said. "I heard something . . ."

*Yip! Yip!*

"Hey!" George said. "I heard that too. It sounded like a bark."

"A tiny little bark," Nancy added. "Like's Jennifer's new puppy!"

The sound came again: *Yip! Yip!*

"Come on," Nancy said. "It's coming from this way!"

"Are you crazy?" Bess cried as Nancy and George leaped off the trail and into the woods.

But a moment later Nancy heard Bess's footsteps following them. She guessed her friend was too scared to stay behind by herself.

"BEWARE!" the ghostly voice came again, louder than ever. "YOU MUST TURN BACK NOW, OR ELSE!"

Bess let out a little cry of fear. But Nancy only ran faster toward the voice. She pushed through branches and vines, following the sound.

A second later she burst out of the woods into a different clearing. George and Bess were right behind her.

They all stopped short, out of breath. Five girls and one poodle puppy stood staring back at them.

"What are you doing here?" Alison Wegman asked, sounding annoyed and a little embarrassed.

Nancy looked around. Standing next to Alison, she saw Sarah Churnichan, Lindsay Mitchell, and Laura McCorry. Jennifer was also there, standing a little bit behind them with Princess in her arms. The puppy let out a loud *Yip!* and wriggled to get free. Nancy noticed that the poodle was wearing a tiny, sparkly barrette in the curly hair on her head. Suddenly she realized it was almost exactly the same as the one they had just found on the trail!

Nancy also saw that Laura was holding a megaphone. She pointed to it. "So that's how you made your voice sound ghostly," she said.

Laura glanced down at the megaphone. She looked sheepish. "It's my older brother's," she said. "He uses it for football practice."

Meanwhile, George was staring around the clearing. "Wow," she commented. "You guys brought a lot of stuff out here."

Nancy saw that George was right. A large flashlight was sitting on the ground nearby, along with a bag of potato chips, some soda bottles, and a stack of magazines. There were even a couple of folding chairs. One of them held a small, battery-powered radio.

"So it was you guys all along!" Nancy exclaimed. "You've been hiding out here in the woods trying to scare people. But why?"

Alison crossed her arms across her chest and looked grumpy. But Sarah and Jennifer traded an embarrassed glance.

Then Jennifer spoke up. "I guess we might as well tell them."

"No!" Alison snapped. "It's a secret."

"Not anymore," Lindsay pointed out. She looked at Nancy. "See, we started this secret club. It's called the Five Friends Club, or FFC for short."

Nancy's eyes widened as she remembered the song she'd heard them singing. Before she could say anything, Laura spoke up.

"We didn't want anyone to find our secret meeting spot," she said, waving one hand at the clearing. "So we started trying to scare people away by making them think the woods were haunted."

"It was just sort of a joke at first," Jennifer added. "We just told people some spooky stories, and pretty soon everyone was talking about it. But then when we heard you were trying to solve the mystery, we decided we should do some scarier stuff."

Sarah rolled her eyes. "Especially after Jennifer accidentally called your puppy with her new dog whistle yesterday. We were afraid you would find us for sure. So we came up with some really good ideas— like making spooky sounds through the megaphone, and calling Jason and those guys pretending to be ghosts."

Nancy nodded. Most of the mysterious events were starting to make sense. Even the mismatched footprints seemed perfectly ordinary now that she realized they weren't mismatched at all. They were left by two different girls wearing different pairs of sneakers.

But one thing still puzzled her. "But why?" she asked. "Why did you want to start a secret club like that in the first place?"

All five girls were silent. They looked at each other. Alison still looked grumpy.

Finally, Lindsay spoke up. "It was *her* idea," she said, pointing to Alison. "She's having a fight with Brenda Carlton. So she thought we'd start the club to prove she's more popular than Brenda."

Alison gasped. "That's not true," she cried. "You guys thought it was a good idea too."

Just then there was a shout from nearby. "Here they are!"

A second later a whole group of kids trooped into the clearing. Brenda was at the front of the group. Jason and his friends were there too.

"We came to rescue you," Jason said to Nancy and her friends. "We heard that spooky voice again and figured you girls needed a bunch of guys like us to help you out."

George rolled her eyes. "Is that why you let Brenda lead the way?" she joked.

Meanwhile, Brenda was staring at Alison.

70

"What are you guys doing here?" she cried. "Are you the ones who've been trying to scare everyone?"

Most of the other kids heard her. They started murmuring and were all staring at Alison. Alison kept quiet, but the other members of the FFC started apologizing and trying to explain. The chatter in the clearing grew louder and louder as everyone found out what had happened.

Nancy stepped forward. "Alison," she said, "I think your plan backfired. Instead of making you *more* popular, the FFC made you way *less* popular."

Alison scowled. "I don't care," she said stubbornly.

But Nancy didn't believe her. Alison looked so upset that Nancy felt sorry for her.

"It's okay," she said kindly, putting a hand on Alison's arm. "Everyone makes mistakes. Maybe you could invite everyone to join your club."

"Nobody wants to do that," Alison mumbled. "Everyone's mad at me now. I'm sorry."

Brenda heard her. She smiled uncertainly. "I'm not mad at you, Alison," she said. "Not anymore. Can I be in your club?"

Alison looked surprised. "Um, sure!" she said. "Everyone can be in it."

"But then it won't make sense to call it the Five Friends Club anymore," Lindsay pointed out.

Alison smiled. "That's okay," she said. "Maybe we can call it the Fabulous Friends Club instead."

Everyone cheered. "Come on," Nancy said. "Let's all go back to the park."

Alison and Brenda linked arms with each other and led the way down the trail. Jennifer, Lindsay, Sarah, and Laura were right behind them. Nancy followed with her two best friends.

"Another case closed," Bess said. "I'm glad it wasn't real ghosts!"

Nancy nodded. She was thinking over the whole case. Almost everything made sense now. There was just one thing still bugging her.

"I guess this means all our suspects are innocent," she said. "But it still doesn't explain why Mr. Garrison is so grumpy

all the time. I guess Hannah is wrong and he just doesn't like kids after all."

"I guess so," George agreed. "Too bad for us."

Just then they reached the edge of the woods. Nancy stepped out onto the soccer field just in time to see Mr. Garrison walking by.

"Oops," Bess whispered with a giggle. "I hope he didn't hear us talking about him."

Meanwhile, Jennifer set Princess down on the ground. The poodle puppy let out a *Yip!* and raced up to Mr. Garrison, her tiny tail wagging.

"Aaah!" Mr. Garrison cried fearfully as the puppy leaped up on his leg. "Get that thing away from me! Get it away!"

Without waiting for an answer, he turned and raced off at top speed. Princess followed for a few steps, then gave up.

Nancy's eyes widened. She thought back on the other times she'd seen Mr. Garrison. She realized he only seemed grumpy when Chip was off her leash—or when he thought she was.

"Did you see that?" she exclaimed. "I think

we just solved the last piece of the mystery."

"What's that?" George asked.

Nancy smiled. "Mr. Garrison isn't grumpy," she said. "He's just afraid of dogs!"

A little later, as her friends played with Princess, Nancy sat down on the grass by herself. She pulled out her detective notebook and her pen and started to write.

We just solved the Secret in the Spooky Woods. But the real secret turned out to be Alison Wegman's club. I guess she knows now that clubs are more fun if you share them with lots of people.

I also found out that even adults can have secrets—like Mr. Garrison. This whole time we thought he was a big grump. But he was just scared to death of dogs!

Anyway, I'm definitely going to be nicer to him from now on. I think Alison and Brenda are going to be nicer to each other, too. At least for a while!

Case closed!